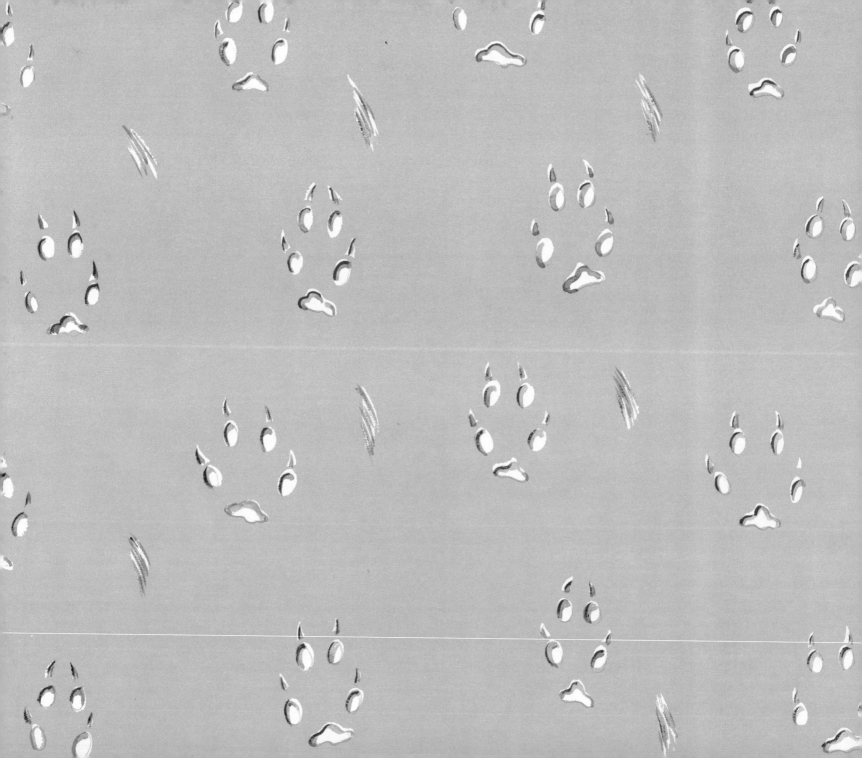

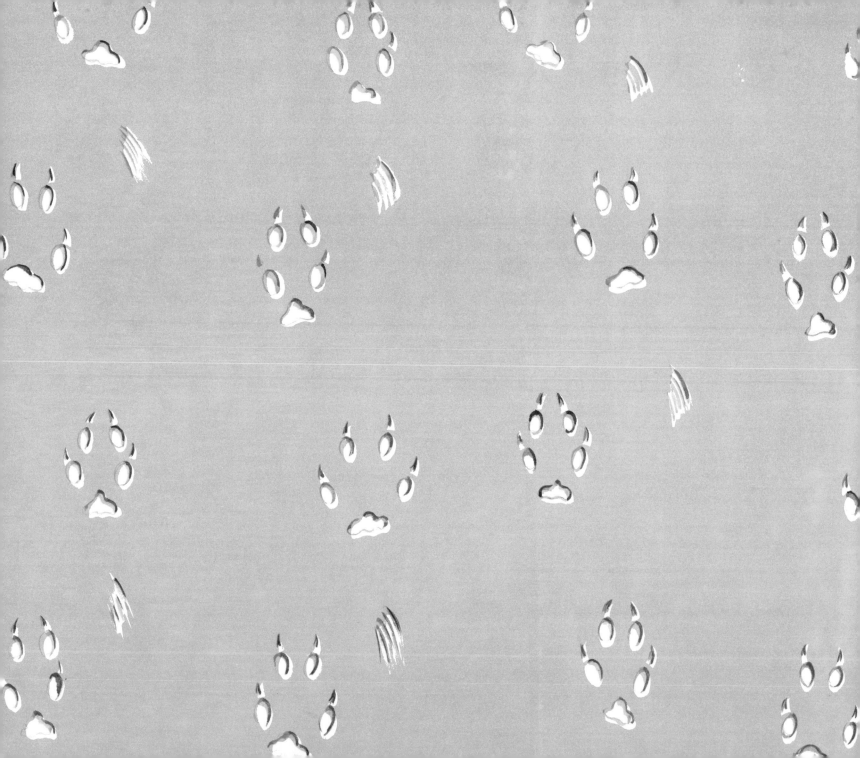

To Campbell,
who also likes to ski

ROGER AND THE FOX

by Lavinia R. Davis

Pictures by Hildegard Woodward

DOUBLEDAY & COMPANY, INC. — GARDEN CITY, N. Y.

ISBN: 0-385-07471-9 TRADE
0-385-07653-3 PREBOUND

15   14   13   12   11

The fall wind swished through the leaves of the trees. The leaves floated to the ground like little umbrellas. And the wind, still chasing and teasing, rolled and tossed them across the road. Roger's feet, in his new school shoes, scuffled through the dried leaves.

Rustle-rustle-crack went the leaves. Roger, who was six, and walking home from school, grinned to himself. He loved the sound of rustling leaves. It was a fine, dry, corn-popping, pie-eating, cider-drinking, *fall* sound.

At the bend in the road the wind died down. Roger heard another noise. It was a little, shy, scurrying noise deep in the leaves. Roger started forward. Then he remembered what Seth had said and he stood still as a fence post and waited. Seth was the hired man on Roger's father's farm and he knew everything.

"If you want to see wild animals," Seth had said, "you can't just rush in on 'em. You have to wait and be patient."

This time Roger didn't have to wait long. There was another stir in the leaves, and then, plain as a pumpkin, out came the chipmunk and darted across the road.

Roger hurried home to tell Seth. He stayed at the house only long enough to help himself to ginger cookies and then he ran up to the barn.

Seth was milking when Roger told him about the chipmunk. "I saw it all by myself," Roger said. "I just stood still and I saw it."

Seth went right on squirting milk into the pail. "Saw a big fox myself this morning," he said finally. "Fine red one down at the river by that ironwood tree that was blown over in the hurricane."

"A fox!" said Roger, and suddenly he felt as flat as a pricked balloon. What was a little old chipmunk compared to a fine red fox?

Roger left the barn and went straight down the long hill toward the Still River. Roger wanted to see that fox himself. Since he and his family had moved to the farm he had seen squirrels, rabbits, field mice, turtles, and of course chipmunks. Once from a safe distance his big brother Dick had shown him a skunk. But until today Roger hadn't even been sure that there were foxes in Connecticut.

Even after Roger reached the river he had a long walk ahead of him. The cold black water twisted and turned between the trees like a pretzel. It was damp and chilly walking along the riverbank, and Roger began to rustle leaves again because the sound made him feel warmer.

It was nearly dark by the time Roger reached the fallen-down tree where Seth had seen the fox. He looked and looked. He couldn't see a thing except the big ironwood tree arching over the river like a shadowy bridge. Roger was colder than ever now and hungry, and there wasn't so much as ginger dust left from his cookies. Pretty soon he started for home. He'd come back tomorrow and bring Scamper with him. Scamper was a fox terrier and almost as smart as Seth's coon hound, Ranger. Roger felt sure if he had Scamper along he'd see the fox.

There was always a lot to do after school, and it was more than two weeks before Roger finally took Scamper down to the long hill to look for the fox.

When he did go, the river looked colder than ever. Even Scamper shivered with cold and then shot through the woods, running as fast as he could to keep warm. By the time Roger caught up with him he was already at the fallen-down tree, yipping and barking and snuffing the ground.

"Be quiet, Scamper!" Roger said, but it didn't do a bit of good. Scamper barked louder than ever. Roger was just going to scold again when he saw the hole! It was quite a big hole and half hidden by the fallen-down tree. Roger's heart beat faster and faster as he looked at that hole. He knew, he just knew, that that was the fox's front porch.

Scamper snuffed and pawed at the hole and Roger looked and looked, but they didn't see a thing. The fox had heard Scamper's barks and Roger's shouts and he didn't so much as put his nose out.

"Come on home," Roger said finally, and now he felt very cross with Scamper. "You made too much noise. Ranger would have had more sense."

After that Roger didn't get down to the river for a long while because every time he started out Scamper came after him. He tried shutting Scamper up, but somebody always let him out and then he was noisier than ever.

Finally one Saturday Dick started to teach Scamper tricks and then Roger knew he was safe. He hurried right down to the river, and this time he went very quietly indeed.

He walked through the woods without even rustling a leaf, but he hadn't counted on the crows. He didn't even see the crows sitting in the birches and the oak trees and the thorn apples. But the crows saw Roger. All of a sudden they began to caw, caw, CAW, and flew off, flapping their great black wings. They were so noisy and so un-expected that Roger jumped! The fox

must have jumped too! He must have jumped right down into his deep hole because when Roger reached it there was nothing to be seen.

The very next Saturday Roger started off right after breakfast to try to see the fox.

"Seen the fox yet?" Seth asked as he passed the barn. Roger shook his head, but he didn't say a word. He wasn't going to take a chance by boasting to Seth, but in his heart he felt that this would be his lucky day. Scamper was off on a hunting trip of his own, the weather was warmer, he himself had just finished a specially good breakfast, and he just felt like fooling that fox.

Roger walked on tiptoes until he was near the fallen-down tree. Then he hid behind an oak tree and peered cautiously out at the fox hole. He looked at the hole and then he took a deep, excited breath! There was something big and reddish-brown. Was it—surely it must be—the fox?

Roger never had a chance to make sure. Just at that moment a big pointer dog jumped through the brush. Right behind him were three duck hunters with their guns under their arms. Roger started forward with his finger on his lips, but it was no use. He had forgotten the cat briers that grew along the river-bank. The next instant Roger tripped over a cat brier and fell flat in front of the hunters!

"Well, sonny," said one of the hunters when they had picked him up and made sure he wasn't hurt, "what are you doing out so early?"

"Fox!" panted Roger, and nodded toward the hole. The three hunters looked and Roger looked, but there wasn't anything there. Even the pointer just sniffed the hole and then went down toward the river looking for duck. "But—but I saw it!" Roger began. "At least I think——"

"Sure, sonny." The biggest hunter grinned down at Roger. "When I was your size I used to see lions and tigers and giraffes in these woods."

Roger knew when he was being teased, so he started for home. As he walked up the long hill he knew it wasn't his lucky day after all. He didn't mind tripping over the cat brier. He didn't mind the hunter's teasing. What he did mind was that he couldn't honestly be sure if he had seen the fox or just imagined him. And if he told that to Seth he knew he'd be laughed at and he would mind that most of all.

Soon after that the Christmas vacation began and Roger was very busy making his presents. Then the day after Christmas Roger caught a bad cold and had to stay in bed. He spent the time drawing pictures of the fallen-down tree with his new Christmas paints and tracing the outline of a fox in one of his new books. And all the time he wished that the weather would clear up and his cold go away so that he could get back to the river and make sure about the fox.

Roger's cold was soon gone, but the weather wasn't in any hurry to get better. First it rained, then it froze, and then it rained some more. Finally a day came when it was clear and dry, and Roger was well enough to put on his new snow suit and rubber boots and go outside. He felt nice and warm as he started down for the river, but he also felt a bit stiff because the suit and the boots were so very new.

When Roger reached the river the bank was all covered with gleaming sheets of melted-then-frozen snow. It was fine and flat and glistening and just made to be jumped on. Roger took his first jump, and the thin sheet of ice cracked and splintered. He took another jump and listened to the crackle. He jumped again. It was a wonderful noise. It was a sharp, biting, where-are-my-mittens, *midwinter* noise.

Roger jumped almost all the way to the fallen-down tree. It was great fun, but it wasn't the way to see a fox. The fox must have heard all that cracking and splintering a long way off because by the time Roger reached his home no one was there.

There was nothing for Roger to do but turn around and walk up the long, steep hill toward home. He was very tired when he reached the top, and his beautiful new snow suit had rubbed chapped places under his knees.

Seth came out of the barn just as Roger passed it on his way to the house. "Seen the fox?" he asked.

"No!" Roger said, and now he was so discouraged he was sure he never would see the fox. "He's always just gone. Always!"

Seth grinned, but his voice was friendly enough. "You have to be real quiet to see a fox," he said. "Quiet and mighty quick. It wouldn't be easy for a city boy."

Roger hated being called a city boy and he walked away without saying a word. Someday he was going to see that fox all by himself. He just had to see it!

The next day it was Roger's seventh birthday, and that was so exciting he almost forgot about the fox. Mother and Dad gave him skis. Grandma gave him a box of tin soldiers. Dick gave him a duck whistle. And Seth—well, Seth gave him the very best present of all. It was a cap, a regular Dan'l Boone hunting cap, made out of the skin of a coon that Seth and Ranger had caught.

Roger put on his new snow suit, his new coonskin cap, and his new skis. It was easy to wear the cap. It was easy to wear the snow suit now that the new stiffness had worn off. But it was unexpectedly hard to wear the skis. They were longer than Roger was tall, and when he stood up on them they shot out in different directions.

Roger practiced skiing all that week and all the next week. First he learned to glide in a straight line on the flat snow-covered stretch of lawn behind the house. When there was another snowfall Roger and Dick made a huge snow man called Henriques De Pew, and after a while Roger learned to zigzag on skis around Henriques.

In another ten days Roger even learned how to ski down little hills, though he took a lot of snow baths while he was learning. It was very deep snow indeed, and Roger was glad he had his skis to play with because no one, not even Seth, could have walked down to the river through the thick white drifts.

So Roger kept on practicing, and then one day Dad said he could try the long, steep hill that led down to the river. Dad skied down the hill first, and when he reached the valley he turned and waved. Roger waved back. Daddy looked a long way off, but Roger gave himself a push with his ski poles and started after him.

He flew down that hill so fast that he lost his breath. He just swooped down, but he didn't fall once. "Good boy!" Dad said when he reached the valley. "That's skiing."

Well, of course, after that Roger didn't want to stop skiing. Even after Dad left to cut wood he kept right on skiing by himself up and down the long, steep hill. It was hard work zigzagging up to the top, but it was worth it to come zooming down again.

It was quite late, and Roger had just reached the valley after a specially good run when he heard the far-off tinkling of a big cowbell. Roger knew that Mother was ringing that cowbell because it was suppertime.

Roger zigzagged up the hill for the last time. Now that the bell had stopped ringing the world seemed quieter than ever. There were no voices, no crows, no dogs to bark. There was only the cold, lonely wail of the wind in the telephone wires and the faint squeak-squeak of his own ski harnesses.

When Roger reached the hilltop he looked back proudly at the fine, clean tracks his skis had made on all his runs downhill. The snow was pale blue and purple now in the fading light, and the tracks stood out clear and bold.

Roger turned away and skied cross-country toward the house. He was just sliding down the last little slope to the front door when Mother came out to ring the bell again. She had just lifted up the bell when Roger snow-plowed to a stop beside her. She was so surprised she jumped and dropped the bell in the snow.

"Why, Rog!" she said. "You did surprise me. I didn't hear you coming at all!"

When she said that Roger had a wonderful idea. If he had surprised Mother he could surprise the fox! At last he'd found a way to go places that was very fast and very quiet and, what was more, the deep drifts wouldn't bother him a bit. Tomorrow he'd put on his snow suit, his hunting cap, *and* his skis and just fool that fox.

It snowed while **Roger** and **Dick** made popcorn that evening. It snowed while they were asleep. It snowed and snowed great, soft, white flakes that covered up the bushes, and covered up the dog kennel, and covered up the fences so that only the tops of the tallest fence posts stuck out like little black rabbit ears.

When Roger woke up the next morning the ceiling in his room glistened with reflected light. Roger lay still for a moment under his patchwork quilts and blinked up at the brightness. Then slowly he understood. There was more new snow. Piles and drifts of it, and he could ski soundlessly over it all and surprise Mr. Fox!

When Roger reached the top of the long hill again there wasn't a single sign of a living creature and there wasn't a sound either. The ski tracks he had made yesterday were gone, and no wind whistled through the telephone wires. There was nothing but new snow and the breathless quiet of the hill listening to itself.

Roger pulled down his coonskin cap and hugged himself because he was so glad he was the first person out in that brand-new world. He felt like a real hunter now, a frontiersman, a breaker of trails.

Roger pushed off and sifted soundlessly down the long, steep hill to the river valley. He never stopped until he reached the wood lot nearest the fallen-down tree. Then he stood so still that even Henriques De Pew, the snow man, seemed like a jitterbug in comparison. There, straight ahead of Roger's nose, was the fox standing beside his hole!

The fox's head was up, his bushy tail was out like a flag. Except for the slight twitching of his whiskers, he was just as still as Roger himself!

All of a sudden the fox put back his head and barked. It didn't sound like Scamper or Ranger. It sounded like nothing on earth but a big, red fox, and it was the wildest, eeriest sound Roger had ever heard.

Only Roger's eyeballs moved as he saw the second fox come out of the hole. She was smaller and lighter-colored and more timid-looking than the first fox. By this time Roger was so excited he was shaking! He took a step forward to balance himself, and the tip of one ski hit into a tree trunk and knocked the snow from its branches. There wasn't much noise. Just the very soft plopping sound of snow from the trees falling onto snow on the ground. It was hardly a noise at all, but it was enough!

The two foxes disappeared!

One moment they were right there in front of Roger and the next they were not. They had melted away faster than the noise of an exploded firecracker. Roger stared, and then a grin spread from one side of his coonskin cap all the way to the other side. Right before him where the foxes had stood were new, clear tracks in the snow. Roger looked at the tracks and looked again. The tracks were fox paw prints and they were right where he had seen the foxes!

After that Roger did not wait another minute. He made a kick turn and started straight up the hill to tell Seth. This time he hadn't been fooled. He had seen the fox and there were paw prints to prove it. More than that, he had seen two foxes, which was just twice as many as Seth himself had seen!

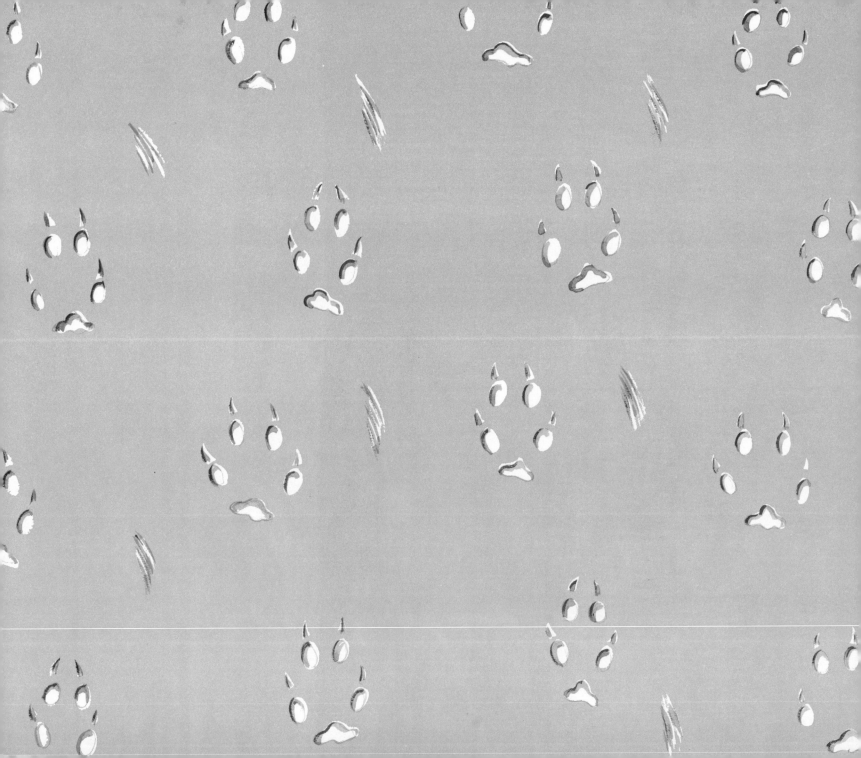

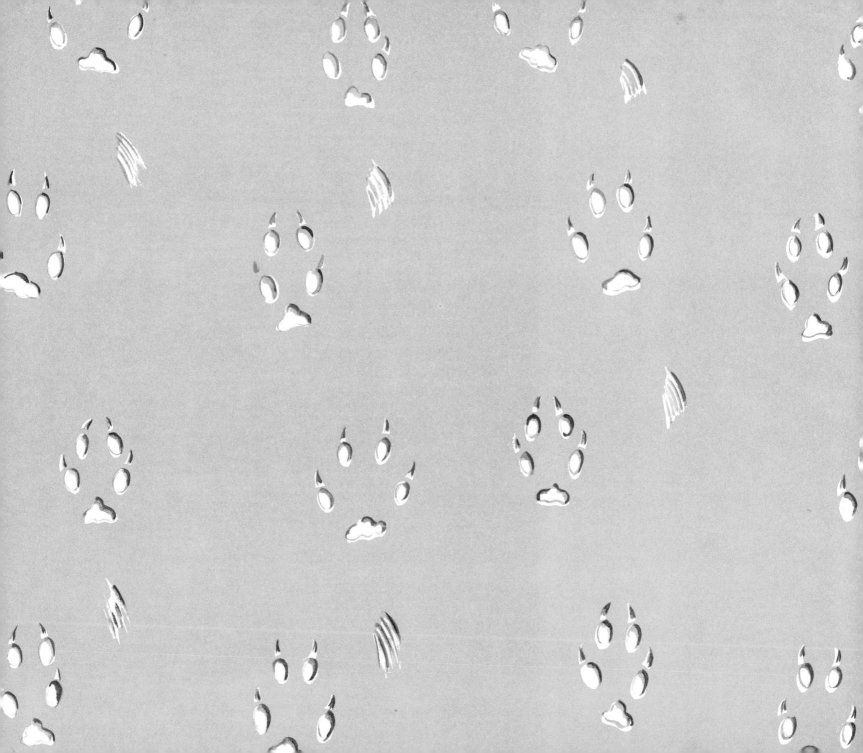